For Madeline, Finn, Eli, Noah, and Gordon

Special thanks to John Candell, Michael Duffy, Emily Easton,
and Donna Mark for helping me with this book

First published in the United States of America in October 2011
by Walker Publishing Company, Inc., a division of Bloomsbury Publishing, Inc.
www.bloomsburykids.com

For information about permission to reproduce selections from this book, write to
Permissions, Walker BFYR, 175 Fifth Avenue, New York, New York 10010

Library of Congress Cataloging-in-Publication Data
McLimans, David.
Big Turtle / by David McLimans.
p.   cm.
Summary: In the time when all people live in the sky and all animals in the water, Sky Girl falls through a hole, is rescued by swans
and taken to wise Big Turtle who, with the help of noble Toad, called Mashutaha, creates the land on which we live.
Includes notes about the Huron people from whom the tale comes.
Includes bibliographical references.
ISBN 978-0-8027-2282-9 (hardcover) • ISBN 978-0-8027-2283-6 (reinforced)
[1. Toads—Folklore. 2. Turtles—Folklore. 3. Wyandot Indians—Folklore. 4. Indians of North America—Folklore.] I. Title.
PZ8.1.M4654Big 2011   597.8'7—dc23   2011010586

Illustrations created using pencil, pen, tracing paper, and computer
Typeset in Whitney
Book design by John Candell

Printed in China by C&C Offset Printing Co., Ltd., Shenzhen, Guangdong
2 4 6 8 10 9 7 5 3 1 (hardcover)
2 4 6 8 10 9 7 5 3 1 (reinforced)

All papers used by Bloomsbury Publishing, Inc., are natural, recyclable products
made from wood grown in well-managed forests. The manufacturing processes
conform to the environmental regulations of the country of origin.

BIG TURTLE

David McLimans

WALKER & COMPANY   NEW YORK

Long ago, the World had two parts.

All the people lived above in the Sky World.

And all the animals lived below in the Water World.

One day after breakfast, Sky Girl took a very long walk.

She walked and walked but quickly tired because she was going to have twins. She was so tired she couldn't take another step.

So Sky Girl decided to take a nap.

She lay down under an apple tree and fell fast asleep.

Suddenly, the ground began to rumble,
and a big hole opened up next to her.
"What's happening?" screamed Sky Girl.

In a flash, the apple tree and the girl
were pulled down into the hole.

Down, down, down tumbled Sky Girl.

Two swans saw her falling. One yelled, "Let's catch her!"
"We must move quickly!" shouted the other.
The two swans spread their wings and caught her just
before she hit the water.

"Phew! That was close. But what am I to do now?" asked Sky Girl. "I can't get back to the Sky World, and I can't live in the water."

"Don't worry. We'll take you to see Big Turtle. He'll know what to do," said one of the swans.

After hearing what happened, Big Turtle called a meeting of all the animals. He told them there was special soil deep down beneath the water.

"If one of you can bring up some of the soil, we can use it to build an island on my back for Sky Girl to live on," said Big Turtle.

"That sounds like a good plan to me," said Sky Girl.
"Thank you all for your help."

Then Beaver, Muskrat, and Otter started arguing.

"I can do it," said Beaver.

"No, I can do it," said Muskrat.

"Don't be silly," said Otter. "I can certainly dive deepest!"

"Aaachooo!"

sneezed Sky Girl. "These feathers are making my nose itch, so please hurry."

Just then, Toad popped out of the water and said,
"I can do it. I can dive deeper than any of you."

Muskrat, Beaver, and Otter just laughed, and Beaver said,
"Toad, you're too small and weak to dive that deep."

"Quiet!" shouted Big Turtle.

"Everyone has a special skill, and everyone
will have a chance to try."

"I'll go first," said Muskrat, before anyone could argue, and down he dived. They waited, but when Muskrat surfaced, he had no soil.

"Now I'll try," said Beaver, and down he dived. They waited and waited, but Beaver came up with nothing.

"I'll go next," said Otter, and down he dived. They waited and waited, full of hope, but Otter came up empty.

"Okay, it's my turn," said Toad, and down she dived.
They waited for a very long time, so long that they
worried they might never see her again.

Suddenly Toad surfaced, leaped out of the water,
and spat a mouthful of soil on Big Turtle's back.
At first, everyone cheered!

But then they saw how exhausted she was, and to
their horror, poor Toad fell back into the water dead.

"Hurry!"
ordered Big Turtle.
"Don't waste Toad's sacrifice!"

Muskrat, Beaver, and Otter jumped on Big Turtle's back and spread the soil around.

All over Big Turtle's shell, things began to grow.

They grew and grew until an island formed
that was big enough for Sky Girl to live on.

It grew into the world we know today. And the descendants of Sky Girl became the Earth's First People.

To this day, Big Turtle carries the Earth on his back. When he gets tired and needs to stretch or change position, we feel the earth quake.

Toad is still honored today. Native Americans call her Mashutaha, which means Our Grandmother. No one is allowed to harm her descendants, in remembrance of her sacrifice.

Big Turtle is a Huron American Indian creation myth. People in many different parts of the world have creation myths. The stories and characters vary from culture to culture, but they all explain how people came to live on Earth, and celebrate their vital, holistic, and sacred relationship with nature.

When French traders arrived in North America around 1535, the Huron, or Wendat, people lived near Lake Huron in southern Ontario. They lived according to the cycles of the seasons and were completely dependent on the natural world for survival. The sun, moon, earth, water, plants, animals, and everything else around them were sacred, and they celebrated this bond with nature through festivals, dances, and stories. Animals were highly regarded and possessed special knowledge and power. In many stories, as in *Big Turtle*, animals played a major role and often talked to humans.

In Wisconsin, where I live, we are surrounded by water, and the Great Lakes dominate this amazing freshwater world. As a boy, I loved to play in this watery wonderland, and it is where I formed a deep connection with nature. We are also surrounded by Native American place names: Manitowoc, Kewaunee, Shawano, Waupaca, Sheboygan, Oconto, Wonewoc, and Mazomanie, to name a few. The Oneida, Menominee, Potawatomi, Ho-Chunk, Mohican, and Ojibwe tribes still hold land here, but it is a tiny proportion of the land they once had. Seeing and hearing these Native American words remind me of the tragic story of the relationship between Native and non-Native people over the past five hundred years, but they also remind me of the connection that Native people have to the natural world.

Indigenous people worldwide continue to lose ground, as well as plants, animals, and the ecosystems that support them. In many ways our planet is suffering and in need of repair. Science and technology have brought us many wonderful insights and devices, but unless we protect and restore our most basic resources, the health of the planet will continue to decline.

I am grateful for Native myths that have been passed from generation to generation, and I'm honored to have had the opportunity to illustrate *Big Turtle*. It seems impossible for all people to see the world in the same way, but if we look closely and carefully, it is not impossible to see that we are all connected to the same world.

Treat the Earth well. It was not given to you by your parents, it was loaned to you by your children.
We do not inherit the Earth from our ancestors, we borrow it from our children.
—Native American proverb

SOURCES

Books

Bial, Raymond. *The Huron.* Lifeways. Tarrytown, NY: Marshall Cavendish, 2000.

Bonvillain, Nancy. *The Huron.* New York: Chelsea House, 1989.

Libal, Autumn. *Huron.* North American Indians Today. Broomall, PA: Mason Crest, 2003.

Lowenstein, Tom. *Mother Earth, Father Sky: Native American Myth.* Myth and Mankind.
  New York: Time-Life Books, 1998.

Murdoch, David. *North American Indian.* Eyewitness Books. New York: DK, 2005.

Suzuki, David, and Peter Knudtson. *Wisdom of the Elders: Sacred Native Stories of Nature.*
  New York: Bantam, 1993.

Taylor, Colin F., and William C. Sturtevant, eds. *The Native Americans: The Indigenous People of North America.*
  San Diego, CA: Salamander Books, 1991.

Museums

HEARD MUSEUM
2301 N. Central Avenue
Phoenix, AZ 85004
602-252-8848
www.heard.org

MASHANTUCKET PEQUOT MUSEUM AND
RESEARCH CENTER
110 Pequot Trail, P.O. Box 3180
Mashantucket, CT 06338-3180
800-411-9671
www.pequotmuseum.org

MITCHELL MUSEUM OF THE AMERICAN INDIAN
3001 Central Street
Evanston, IL 60201
847-475-1030
www.mitchellmuseum.org

NATIONAL MUSEUM OF THE AMERICAN INDIAN
www.nmai.si.edu
(two sites):

NMAI on the National Mall in Washington DC
Fourth Street & Independence Ave., S.W.
Washington DC 20560
202-633-1000

NMAI in New York City
The George Gustav Heye Center
Alexander Hamilton U.S. Custom House
One Bowling Green
New York, NY 10004
212-514-3700

Websites

AMERICAN INDIAN LIBRARY ASSOCIATION www.ailanet.org

FIRST PEOPLE OF AMERICA AND CANADA www.firstpeople.us

INDEX OF NATIVE AMERICAN RESOURCES ON THE INTERNET www.hanksville.org/NAresources

INSTITUTE OF AMERICAN INDIAN ARTS www.iaiancad.org

LIBRARY OF CONGRESS: INDIANS OF NORTH AMERICA www.loc.gov/rr/main/indians_rec_links/overview.html

NATIVE AMERICAN MYTHS: CREATION BY WOMEN www.crystalinks.com/namcreationwomen.html

NATIVEWEB: RESOURCES FOR INDIGENOUS CULTURES AROUND THE WORLD www.nativeweb.org

PLANET OZ KIDS: ANIMALS, MYTHS & LEGENDS www.planetozkids.com

How to Care for Your "Other" Circulatory System

Andrew L. Rubman, ND, medical director of the Southbury Clinic for Traditional Medicines in Southbury, Connecticut.

Your body's ability to resist infections depends on a healthy lymphatic system, which drains excess fluids and captures (and kills) cancer cells, bacteria and viruses. But immunity, it turns out, may be only part of what this system does.

Intriguing new finding: For the first time, scientists have identified a "shadow" plumbing system that rapidly drains wastes from the brain. Age- or injury-related damage to the glymphatic system (named for the glial cells in the brain) could impair drainage and contribute to many neurodegenerative diseases, including Alzheimer's disease. *Key facts about the lymphatic system…*

SLUGGISH CIRCULATION

After blood delivers nutrients to the body's tissues, it "leaks" into the empty spaces between cells. The lymphatic system picks up this fluid (now stripped of red blood cells) and returns it to the circulation. Along the way, it passes through one or more of the body's hundreds of lymph nodes, which are packed with infection-fighting immune cells. The lymphatic system also includes the adenoids, tonsils, thymus and spleen. What happens when this system becomes overworked or "congested"? You might notice that some of your lymph nodes—in your neck, under the chin, in the armpits, etc.—are swollen and tender. This usually indicates that an infection is brewing in a nearby area of the body. Your legs or arms also could feel puffy and bloated or swollen—a sign that lymphatic fluid is accumulating faster than it can be removed.

During a routine checkup, your doctor will feel for swollen lymph nodes in the neck, in front of the ears and around the armpits and groin, etc. Swelling and/or tenderness means that drainage is impaired.

Examples: Swollen lymph nodes in the groin area could mean that you have a pelvic or urinary tract infection. Swelling just in front of the ear could indicate an ear infection.

Important: If you notice swollen and/or tender lymph nodes that enlarge or persist for more than a few weeks, see your doctor—even if you have no other symptoms. It could be a sign of an immune system disorder (such as lupus) or cancer.

BETTER DRAINAGE

You're less likely to get an infection—and recover more quickly if you have one—if you follow these steps to help lymph flow efficiently…*

• **Contrast hydrotherapy.** This involves applying heat to an area, followed by immediate exposure to cold. The contrast causes tissues to alternately pump and relax, which pushes fluid through the lymphatic system.

What to do: Let's say that you notice swelling in one or both armpits. Soak a washcloth in water that's about 104°F—the temperature of a hot bath. Apply it to the area for three to five minutes, continuing to reheat the cloth when it starts feeling cool. Next, soak a cloth in ice water and apply it to the same area for a minute or two, then switch back to heat. Repeat the cycle three to five times, and do it three times a day until the swelling goes down. If there's no improvement within a few weeks, see your doctor.

• **Dry brushing.** Gently passing a brush (or a loofah) over the skin, from the extremities toward the heart (corresponding to the flow of lymphatic fluid), causes the underlying tissues to contract/relax. This pushes accumulated fluid just under the skin into deeper lymphatic vessels. I often recommend dry brushing that includes the face for patients with skin problems that may be caused by congested lymph, such as frequent blackheads.

What to do: Use a high-quality brush, preferably one that's made with natural bristles—it should feel stiff but still have a little "give." Slowly brush the affected area (or the whole

*These therapies are generally safe but should be avoided by people with diabetes or other conditions that impair circulation and cause temperature insensitivities.